D1395600

# OUTSIDERS

By the same author

FICTION

*The Arthur Trilogy:*
*The Seeing Stone*
*At the Crossing-Places*
*King of the Middle March*

STORY COLLECTIONS

*Tales from the Old World*

*The Old Stories: Folk Tales of*
*East Anglia and the Fen Country*

*The Magic Lands: Folk Tales of Britain and Ireland*

*Enchantment: Fairy Tales,*
*Ghost Stories and Tales of Wonder*

*Viking! Myths of Gods and Monsters*

PICTURE BOOKS

*The Ugly Duckling*
(illustrated by Meilo So)

*How Many Miles to Bethlehem?*
(illustrated by Peter Malone)

NON-FICTION

*King Arthur's World*

KEVIN CROSSLEY-HOLLAND

# OUTSIDERS

*Illustrated by*
*Christian Birmingham*

Orion

This collection first published in Great Britain in 2005
by Orion Children's Books
a division of the Orion Publishing Group Ltd
Orion House
5 Upper St Martin's Lane
London WC2H 9EA

A catalogue record for this book is available
from the British Library

Printed in Great Britain by Clays Ltd, St Ives plc

ISBN 1 84255 147 7

www.orionbooks.co.uk

*for Helen and George*

# Contents

Foreword                ix

Sea-Woman                3

The Green Children      17

The Wildman             35

Fine Field of Flax      47

Three Blows             63

Sea Tongue              83

Notes and Sources       97

# Foreword

THINK OF A NECKLACE STRUNG WITH SIX PIECES OF shining glass, each one a different shape and each a different colour, all of them time-smoothed but still sharp-edged. That's how I see these six stories.

There are times when each of us feels like a square peg in a round hole, but in these stories children and adults stand right apart from the communities and places in which they find themselves. They are outsiders, finding out who they are, and whether they can belong. They have to face up to rejection; they win acceptance; no matter what they've lost, they also learn that green time can help and love can heal. They discover what home really means.

Most of these stories are told by the characters

themselves. And most inhabit that strange between-world where earth and water meet. One is Welsh, two are from the northern isles of Britain and three come from East Anglia, my own part of the country.

# Sea-Woman

IT WAS AN EMPTY, OYSTER-AND-PEARL AFTERNOON. The water lipped at the sand and sorted the shingle and lapped round the rock where the girl was sitting.

Then she saw a seal, like a mass of seaweed almost, until she gazed into those eyes. It swam in quite close, just twenty or thirty water-steps away.

She looked at the sea; the seal looked at her. Then it barked. It cried out in a loud voice.

She stood up on her rock. She called out to the seal: not a word but a sound, the music words are made of.

The seal swam in a little closer. It looked at the girl. Then it cried. Oh! The moon's edge and a mother's ache were in that cry.

The girl jumped off the rock. Her eyes were sea-eyes, wide and flint-grey. 'Seal!' she cried. 'Sea-woman! What do you want?'

And what did the seal want but the girl's company?

As she padded down the strand, it followed her, always keeping fifteen or twenty water-steps away, out in the dark swell. The girl turned back towards her rock, and the seal turned with her. Sometimes it huffed and puffed, sometimes it cried, it wailed as if it were lost, all at sea.

The girl bent down and picked up a curious shell, opaline and milky and intricate.

'Listen, listen!' sang the wind in the shell's mouth.

Then the girl raised the shell and pressed it to her right ear.

❧

'One afternoon,' sang the shell, 'oyster-and-pearl, a man came back from the fishing. He was so weary. He peeled off his salt-stiff clothing. He washed. For an hour or two hours he closed his eyes. And then, when the moon rose, he came strolling along this strand.

'He listened to the little waves kissing in the rocks. He smelt earth on the breeze and knew it would soon rain. This is where he walked, rocking slightly from side to side, in no hurry at all for there was nowhere to go.

'Then he stopped. Down the beach, no more than

the distance of a shout, he saw a group of sea-people dancing. They were singing and swaying; they danced like the waves of the sea.

'Then the sea-people saw him. At once they stopped singing and broke their bright ring. As the fisherman began to run towards them, they turned towards a pile of sealskins – in the moonlight they looked like a wet rock – and picked them up and pulled them on and plunged into the water.

'One young woman was not so quick, though. She was so caught up in the dance that the fisherman reached her skin before she did. He snatched it up and tucked it under one arm. Then he turned to face the sea-woman, and he was grinning.

'"Please," she said. Her voice was high as a handbell and flecked with silver. "Please."

'The fisherman shook his head.

'"My skin," said the sea-woman. There she stood, dressed in moonlight, reaching out towards him with her white arms; and he stood between her and the sea.

'"I've landed some catches," breathed the fisherman, "but never anything like this . . ."

'Then the young woman began to sob. "I cannot," she cried, "I cannot go back without my skin."

5

'*. . . and this catch I'll keep*, thought the fisherman.

'"My home, said the sea-woman. "My family and my friends,"

'Now she wept and the moon picked up her salt tears and turned them into pearls. How lovely she was, and lovely in more ways than one: a young woman lithe as young women are, a sea-child, a sister of the moon. For all her tears, the fisherman had not the least intention of giving her back her skin.

'"You'll come with me," he said.

'The sea-woman shuddered.

'Then the man stepped forward and took her by the wrist. "Home with me," he said.

'The sea-woman neither moved towards the man nor pulled away from him. "Please," she said, her voice sweet and ringing. "The sea is my home, the shouting waves, the green light and the darkening."

'But the fisherman had set his heart against it. He led the sea-woman along the strand and into the silent village and back to his home.

'Then the fisherman shut the door on the sea-woman and went out into the night again to hide the skin. He waded up to the haystack in the field behind his house, and loosened one of the haybricks and hid the skin behind it. Within ten minutes, he was back on his own doorstep.

'The sea-woman was still there; without her skin, there was nowhere for her to go. She looked at the man. With her flint-grey eyes she looked at him.'

❧

For a moment the girl lowered the shell from her ear. She gazed at the emptiness around her, no one on the beach or on the hill-slope leading down to it, no one between her and the north pole. The little waves were at their kissing and the seal still kept her company, bobbing up and down in the welling water.

'Listen, listen!' sang the wind in the shell's mouth.

The girl raised the shell again and pressed it to her right ear.

❧

'Time passed,' sang the shell, 'and the sea-woman stayed with the fisherman. Without her skin, she was unable to go back to the sea, and the fisherman was no worse than the next man.

'For his part, the fisherman fell in love. He had spent half his life on the ocean. He knew all her moods and movements and colours, and he saw them in the sea-woman.

'Before long the man and the woman married, and they had one daughter and then two sons. The sea-woman loved them dearly and was a good mother to them. They were no different from other children except in one way: there was a thin, half-transparent web between each of their fingers and each of their toes.

'Often the woman came walking along the strand, where the fisherman had caught her. She sat on a rock; she sang sad songs about a happier time; and at times a large seal came swimming in towards her, calling out to her. But what could she do? She talked to the seal in the language they shared; she stayed here for hours; but always, in the end, she turned away and slowly walked back to the village.

'Late one summer afternoon, the sea-woman's three children were larking around on the haystack behind their house. One of the little boys gave his sister a push

from behind, and the girl grabbed wildly at the wall of the haystack.

'One haybrick came away. And the skin, the sealskin that the fisherman had hidden in one stack after another as the years passed, fell to the ground.

'The children stopped playing. They fingered the skin; they buried their faces in its softness; they took it back to show their mother.

'The sea-woman dared scarcely look at it, and looked at it; dared scarcely touch it, and touched it.

'"Mother!" said the children, crowding around her. "What is it?"

'The sea-woman pulled her children to her. She dragged them to her and squeezed them. She hugged and kissed each of them. Then she turned and ran out of the house with her skin.

'The children were afraid. They followed her. They saw her pull on the skin, cry a great cry, and dive off a rock. Then a large seal rose to meet her and the two seals leaped and dipped through the water.

'When their father came back from the fishing, his children were standing at the stone jetty.

'"You go home," said the man. "I'll come back in an hour."

'Slowly the man waded in his salt-stiff clothing

13

along this strand. He kept rubbing his pale blue eyes and looking out across the dancing water.

'She rose out of the waves. She was no more than a few water-steps away.

'"Husband!" she cried. "Husband! Look after our children! Take care of our children!" Her voice carried over the water. "You've loved me and I've loved you. But for as long as I lived with you, I always loved my first husband better."

'Then the sea-woman, the seal-woman, slipped under the sallow waves once more. One moment she was there; the next, she was not there . . .'

❧

The girl took the opaline shell away from her ear, and set it down on the sand. For a long time she sat there. The seal had gone; it had deserted her, and the dark water shivered.

# The Green Children

THIS IS WHAT HAPPENED. ONE OF OUR LAMBS skipped into a dark cave, and we ran in to rescue it. We heard bells in the cave, bright bells, and we stumbled towards them. In and on and up! Up and out of the cave! Away from our home country!

Those bells, they were sunlight, ringing, and the sunlight blinded us.

When my brother and I opened our eyes, we saw faces peering down at us. I looked. The faces were not

green. And the hands and legs, they were not green either.

My little brother pressed his nails into my left arm. 'What are they?' he whispered.

'It's all right,' I replied. 'They're children. Well! I think they are.'

But as soon as we stood up, all the children shuffled backwards. One boy tripped over a tree-root, he bumped his bottom and his brains.

Then they forefingered us and hissed behind their hands. And a little one, I couldn't tell whether it was a boy or a girl, hid its eyes.

'Look!' my brother whispered.

I looked: a boy was cradling berries in a leaf-nest, but they were not green. 'And the birds,' whispered my brother.

A girl was dangling two birds who had lost their songs. But their wings were not green.

Around me, the air was so warm, warm as my own skin, and then it moved. I felt it move! It slipped across my face. I tried to catch it between my hands, and my hair danced.

There was one girl taller than the others; she stepped towards us, half-a-step, and she sang some words.

'What do they mean?' asked my brother.

'I don't know,' I said. 'I've never heard those words. They sound all right.'

Then I asked the girl, 'You, all of you, who are you?'

The tall girl smacked her mouth. She made her eyes dark and wide.

'Why aren't you green?' I asked her. 'Where is this place?'

She gave me her back and whispered with all the children. Then she beckoned, and my brother and I followed her.

❧

The children walked us through a creaking wood. They were in a hurry but we didn't want to hurry. My brother found a marble-stone, and it was quite pale. And I picked a tiny flower, it was shining.

'Look!' we cried. 'Look! I'll take this back. I'll show my father this.'

❧

After we had eaten, we were ready to go home. We touched our noses and our lips to thank the mother – the way our own mother taught us – and stepped out into the beautiful brightness. With the children, we hurried back through the creaking greenwood.

'We'll show them this flower,' I said.

'And this stone,' said my brother. 'That'll prove it.'

But when we walked out of the wood, our way back home had gone. The cave had gone. It wasn't there.

'It must be,' I said. 'Here! This is where we lay down. Here, in this brightness!'

Then my little brother began to cry. We ran hand-in-hand, we looked, we hunted; but the cave had disappeared.

'They will be waiting,' I said.

We didn't want this country then. I dropped the flower, my brother threw away the marble-stone. We put up our flat hands to all the children.

Above our heads, the sky began to change colour! It was so strange: the dark light almost took our eyes from us.

❧

So we had to turn back, we had to sleep with the mother in the hall.

That night. And the next night . . .

Soon the mother began to teach us her words.

'Please,' said my little brother. 'Please we go home.'

After seven days my brother felt ill.

He didn't eat or speak. I knew I should never have led him up to this country.

The children brought him green broth, and the mother sang soft songs.

'He will go home,' I said.

On the ninth evening my brother saw the bright country. He sat straight up, and his eyes were shining.

Then he lay back and the song went out of him. I wrapped him in my warm arms.

❧

That winter I stayed in the hall, and made songs for my brother. Little pieces of the sky fell down to the ground, very pale, very cold.

Each morning the young man came to the hall with more green beans. Sometimes he split them open for me, and he grinned.

'I am Guy,' he said. 'My name is Guy.'

'Guy,' I repeated.

I think he felt awkward inside his body. His arms were so long, his hands were so large; they were the wrong size.

'And you? What is your name?' he asked me.

'I cannot say,' I told him.

Each afternoon the mother sat beside me and gave me more new words.

'I am Alice,' she said. 'My name is Alice.'

So the days passed, one by one; and sound by sound, I learned this strange language.

When it was first spring, Alice called everyone to a feast.

Guy, and the tall girl, the boy who bumped his bottom, the girl with the birds, the boy with the berries: they all came to the feast, and so did many people I had never seen before.

Everyone ate. Then the mother clapped her hands, and I told my story.

❧

'I come from the green country, and it is far below. Where I live, every girl is green. My mother and father, they are green. Everyone is green. The animals are green.'

'What kind of green?' asked Alice.

'I have learned your words,' I said. 'The leaves are lime-green, and willow-green, beech-green. Plants and flowers and trees and stones: they are silver-green and grey-green, leek-green and moss-green, they are jade-green and emerald-green and olive-green. There is no sun to shine. The light in the sky is always quiet and green.

'From up on the high hill, we can see another country, far away from us across the fast, dark river. That is the bright country, where my brother waits.

'My brother and I . . . One of our lambs skipped into a cave, and we ran in to rescue it. It was dark in there, damp wet. And there were eyes!

'Then we heard bright bells, and we followed the bells. In and on and up! Up and out of the cave!'

'That's when we found you,' said the tall girl. 'Green children!'

'Green nails!' said the girl with the birds.

'Pink children!' I replied. 'We'd never heard of pink children before.'

'Green teeth!' said the boy with the berries.

'I have eaten your beans,' I said, 'and you have given me your words. But when I find my way, I must go home.'

'Stay here if you want,' said the boy who bumped his bottom. 'You're green normal.'

'I wish you would as well,' said Guy.

'I must go home,' I said.

'What if you can't?' asked Guy.

'Then here can be home,' said Alice.

❧

Each morning I hunted. I hurried through the greenwood. I kicked leaves and they crackled, I stroked grass and it was silk.

I looked and looked but I couldn't find my way home.

'What if I never do?' I said to myself. 'Where do I belong?'

Time passed, as time does in this country, the seasons and colours changed: charcoal and iron and pearl; then primrose, moon-blue, bud-green.

'Next week is the week of the great fair,' Guy told me.

'What is a fair?' I asked him.

'A market!' said Guy. 'A market and a carnival! We'll walk to town and get good prices for our skins and wool. Spices and salt, silkworms, silver hearts, we'll buy them all.'

'Can I come?' I asked him.

'We'll hurl the stone and bet on the wrestlers and dance with the dancing-bear . . .'

'I'll come,' I said.

But when we reached the town, the fair-people started to forefinger and shout.

'Look at that one!'

'All green!'

'She's a freak!'

'Has she gone rotten?'

'Clear off!' shouted Guy. 'She's normal!'

'How much does she cost?' they yelled. 'How much? Has she got hooves? Has she got nails or claws?'

'Let her be!' shouted Guy. 'She's just the same as you and me.'

'She's a freak!' they screamed. 'She's green!'

I ran away then. I ran out of the town and did not stop running for a long time.

Even then, on my own, the voices of the fair people jeered and hooted and screamed inside my head.

They don't want me here, I thought. I don't belong. I never will.

Guy hunted for me and he found me in the greenwood.

He put a blue flower in my hair; he took my fingers and wrists inside his large, warm hands.

'They don't want me,' I whispered. 'They never will.'

'I love you,' he said, and that is what he said.

'You love me?'

'And here can be home,' he said.

'How can that be?'

'Home is your friends in your own green country. Home is your friends here . . .'

'Both?' I asked.

'Here and there, home is your heart,' cried Guy, and his face was pink and shining. 'Will you stay here with me?'

❧

I walked away then. I wanted to walk on my own. I wanted to think about what Guy had asked me.

And then, in my heart, I found the answer. A bright light grew inside me.

The next day was May Day. Near the hall, Guy and his friends planted a tall pole, hung with fluttering ribbons.

Guy was waiting. Out of the greenwood I walked towards him, and I put my fingers and wrists inside his hands.

'Please!' he said. 'Please tell me!'

'You were right,' I replied, 'and I never knew it. My heart is my home.'

'It is,' said Guy.

'My country and your country, they can both be my home.'

'They can,' said Guy, and all the leaves in the greenwood trembled.

'And when I find my way back . . .' I began. 'I will come with you,' said Guy.

'I am Airha,' I whispered. 'My name is Airha. I will be your green home.'

Guy gave me his arm and I gave him my arm. We ran towards the hall.

Alice and the tall girl, the boy who bumped his bottom, the girl with the birds, the boy with the berries, and many other people: they were waiting for us. They met us with cries and kisses.

Then each of us chose a fluttering ribbon, primrose, moon-blue, green . . . pink . . . Quick, slow, slow, quick, we danced in a ring, we sang and danced our round:

*May Day and morning,*
*This our beginning,*
*Flower faces shining,*
*Green blades now rising.*

*This world is greening,*
*Greening is growing,*
*Growing is living,*
*Living is blessing.*

*Sowing and reaping*
*Through the year's turning,*
*Dying to living,*
*Song without ending.*

# The Wildman

Don't ask me my name. I've heard you have names. I have no name.

❧

They say this is how I was born. A great wave bored down a river, and at the mouth of the river it ran up against a great wave of the sea. The coupled waves kicked like legs and whirled like arms and swayed like hips; sticks in the water snapped like bones and the seaweed bulged like gristle and muscle. In this way the waves rose. When they fell, I was there.

❧

My home is water as your home is earth. I rise to the surface to breathe air, I glide down through the darkening rainbow. The water sleeks my hair as I swim. And when I stand on the sea-bed, the currents comb my waving hair; my whole body seems to ripple.

❦

Each day I go to the land for food. I swim to the shore, I'm careful not to be seen. Small things, mice, shrews, moles, I like them to eat. I snuffle and grub through the growth and undergrowth and grab them, and squeeze the warm blood out of them, and chew them.

❦

Always before sunset I'm back in the tugging, chuckling, sobbing water. Then the blue darkness that comes down over the sea comes inside me too. I feel heavy until morning. If I stayed too long on the land I might be found, lying there, heavy, unable even to drag myself back to the water.

❦

My friends are seals. They dive as I do, and swim as I do. Their hair is like my hair. I sing songs

with their little ones. They've shown me their secret place, a dark grotto so deep that I howled for the pain of the water pressing round me there and rose to the surface, gasping for air. My friends are the skimming plaice and the flickering eel and the ticklish trout. My friends are all the fishes.

❧

As I swam near the river mouth, something caught my legs and tugged at them. I tried to push it away with my hands and it caught my hands and my arms too. I kicked; I flailed; I couldn't escape. I was dragged through the water, up out of the darkness into the indigo, the purple, the pale blue. I was lifted into the air, the sunlight, and down into a floating thing.

❧

Others. There were others in it, others, others as I am. But their faces were not covered with hair. They had very little hair I could see except on their heads, but they were covered with animal skins and furs. When they saw me they were afraid and trembled and backed away, and one fell into the water.

I struggled and bit but I was caught in the web they had made. They took me to land and a great shoal gathered round me there. Then they carried me in that web to a great high place of stone and tipped me out into a gloomy grotto.

❧

One of them stayed by me and kept making noises; I couldn't understand him. I could tell he was asking me things. I would have liked to ask him things. How were you born? Why do you have so little hair? Why do you live on land? I looked at him I kept looking at him, and when the others came back, I looked at them: their hairless hands, their legs, their shining eyes. There were so many of them almost like me, and I've never once seen anyone in the sea like me.

❧

They brought me two crossed sticks. Why? What are they? They pushed them into my face, they howled at me. One of them smacked my face with his hand. Why was that? It hurt. Then another with long pale hair came and wept tears over me. I licked my lips; the tears tasted like the sea. Was this one like me? I put my arms round its waist but it shrieked and pushed me away.

❧

They brought me fish to eat. I wouldn't eat fish. Later they brought me meat; I squeezed it until it was dry and then I ate it.

❧

I was taken out into sunlight, down to the river mouth. The rippling, rippling water. It was pink and lilac and grey; I shivered with longing at the sight of it. I could see three rows of webs spread across the river from bank to bank. Then they let me go, they let me dive into the water. It coursed through my long hair. I laughed and passed under the first web and the second web and the third web. I was free. But why am I only free away from those who are like me, with those who are not like me? Why is the sea my home?

❧

They were all shouting and waving their arms, and jumping up and down at the edge of the water. They were all calling out across the grey wavelets. Why? Did they want me to go back after all? Did they want me to be their friend?

❧

I wanted to go back, I wanted them as friends. So I stroked back under the webs again and swam to the sandy shore. They fell on me then, and twisted my arms, and hurt me. I howled. I screamed. They tied long webs round me and more tightly round me, and carried me back to the place of stone, and threw me into the gloomy grotto.

❧

I bit through the webs. I slipped through the window bars. It was almost night and the blue heaviness was coming into me. I staggered away, back to the water, the waiting dark water.

# Fine Field of Flax

I WILL TELL YOU WHAT I KNOW.

❧

I was born on this island. My mother was born on this island. And her mother and father.

❧

I am part of this place, no less than the green curve of the hill, the twisted tree, the ring of dawn water. We are all part of each other.

❧

She was sixteen when I was born. 'Bonnie,' she murmured, when I fed at her breast. 'Bonnie. Brave.' She was brave and bonnie.

The Northern Lights shook their curtains on the night I was born. Clean and cold and burning.

❧

'And the father,' they said. 'Who is the father? Where is the father?'

❧

She said, 'I cannot tell.'

❧

'Tell me,' whispered her mother. 'Tell me,' ordered her father. 'Tell Mother Church,' hissed the minister. 'What have you to say?'

❧

'There is no more to say,' she said.

❧

Wind sang in the shell; sun danced in the scarlet cup; dew softened the ear.

Days and questions, questions and days. Her mother, her father, her friends, the minister, the elders.

꙳

'I know nothing you do not know,' she said. 'Why do you ask me if you don't believe me?'

꙳

'Out,' they said. 'Away. Out of our sight. You and your issue.'

꙳

We lived in a bothy by the ocean. One room with no cow; it smelt of pine and tar and salt.

꙳

The sea schooled me. I know her changes, her whiplash and switchback and croon. I know the sea-voices, the boom of the bittern, the curlew's cry and the redshank's warning, the shriek of white-tailed sea-eagle and all her sisters. Mine is a sea-voice.

❧

We scratched the sandy wasteland behind the dune and there we sowed our seeds of corn. We picked sea-peas. Sometimes we went hungry.

❧

When we walked into town, they crossed the street to avoid us. 'Slut,' they said. 'Strumpet. Sweet sixteen and a whore.' They spat at us.

❧

I wore rags. What else was there to wear? The sea was my mirror.

❧

'One dress,' said my mother. 'For my daughter. I wish you had one dress.'

I grew up. I grew old. Fourteen, fifteen . . .

❧

Once, I went walking along the cliffs all the way to the edge of the gloup. The black water sluiced and boomed and exploded in the chasm far below.

❧

I waited for a long time. The water moaned and sucked in the long cave that leads out to the sea. Then the gloup was empty.

❧

I wandered up on to the high headland between the gloup and the sea. And there I found it. It was all around me, growing wild, and I grew wild at the sight of it. I swayed with it. I waved with it.

❧

Blue flowers were born after I came. They died before I left.

⚜

I picked the flax. I carried an armful back to the bothy. The next day my mother and I hurried back for more.

⚜

She retted the flax; she scutched and hackled and spun the fibre; she wove the linen. She cut out my dress.

⚜

She culled plants from the green curve and crushed them and boiled them. She scraped bark from the twisted tree. She lit my dress with bright colours. It was so bonnie . . .

⚜

'You're so bonnie,' she told me. 'It becomes you.'

❧

I wore it; my first dress. It sang in the sunlight and danced on the windy dune. Then the laird saw it. He saw the bright signal and rode up. He rode right past our bothy.

❧

Next day it was the laird's son. He stopped and spoke to me. He smiled at me. He talked to my mother.

❧

The laird's son came back with food for us, clothes, gifts. My mother smiled. And when he had gone, she wept and hugged me.

❧

He told me he loved me.

There was a fine wedding. My mother came to live with me in the big house. She lived there and there she died.

I have made you this song;

> *On the ridges two three*
> *between the gloup and the sea*
> *grew a fine field of flax*
> *for my mother and me*
>
> *we picked the flax*
> *on a brave bonnie day*
> *and we jumped in glee*
> *my mother and me*
>
> *the flax we spun*
> *and wove and all*
> *mother made me a gown*
> *so bonnie and brave*

*and the laird when he saw me*
*thought I would do*
*as a wife for his son*
*who was young and gay*
*so we both fell in love*
*and were married one day*

*and it's all because*
*of the ridges two three*
*where the flax grew so bonnie*
*between the gloup and the sea*

*I bore him two sons*
*who travelled afar . . .*
*yet they never forgot*
*the ridges two three*
*where the flax grew so bonnie*
*between the gloup and the sea*

❧

After my mother died, the people on the island began to remember what she had said, and could not say, in the days after I was born. And they began to believe her. Each week they put white flowers on her grave.

There! The Lights have started their dance in the north.

I have told you what I know. You are my children's children's children. All this was long ago.

# Three Blows

THEIR STONE FARMHOUSE SEEMED TO GROW OUT OF THE grey-green skirt of the mountain. The walls were lichenous, one part of the roof was covered with slate and the other part with turf. The whole building seemed to be crouching.

It wasn't alone. Megan could stand at their door (you had to stoop to get in or out) and see three other smallholdings within reach, almost within shouting distance. And no more than a mile away, along the track north and west, was the little huddled village of Llanddeusant.

But when the wind opened its throat and rain swept across the slopes; when the lean seasons came to Black Mountain; when wolves circled the pens and small birds left their sanskrit in the snow: the farm seemed alone then, alone in the world – and all the more so to Megan since her husband had died leaving her to bring up their baby son and run the farm on her own.

But Megan was hard-working. As the years passed, her holding of cattle and sheep and goats increased and strayed far and wide over Black Mountain. And all the while her son grew and grew until he became a big-boned young man: rather awkward, very strong-willed, and shy and affectionate. Sometimes, looking at him sitting by the fire, lost in his own sliding dreams, Megan thought she didn't really know her son. *He's like his father,* she thought. *Something hidden. What's he thinking?*

Gwyn spent most of his time up on Black Mountain, herding the cattle and sheep and goats. More often than not he followed them up to a secret place in a fold of the mountain: the little lake of Llyn y Fan Fach.

One spring morning, Gwyn sat on a flat rock beside the lake and spread out his provisions – barley-bread and a chump of cheese, a wooden bottle seething with ale. He stared out across the lake, silver and obsidian. And there, sitting on the glassy surface of the water, combing her hair, he saw a young woman. She was charming her hair into ringlets, arranging them so that they covered her shoulders; and only when she had finished did she look up and see Gwyn, awkward on the rock, open-mouthed, arms outstretched, offering her bread . . .

Slowly, the young woman rose and glided over the

surface of the water towards Gwyn and, entranced, he stepped down to meet her.

And then Gwyn heard her voice, very sweet and very low. 'Your bread's baked and hard,' she said. 'It's not easy to catch me.'

Which is just what Gwyn tried to do. He lunged into the lake, and at once the girl sank from sight.

For a while Gwyn stood and stared. He felt as if he had lost the one thing in this world that mattered, and he resolved to come back, to catch the girl, whatever the cost.

Gwyn turned away from the lake, and set off down the string-thin sheep-runs. At first he walked slowly, but by the time he reached the doors of his farmhouse he was almost running, so eager was he to tell his mother about the bewitching girl he had seen up at Llyn y Fan Fach.

'Stuff!' said Megan. 'You and your dreams.' But she didn't doubt Gwyn was telling the truth. In the young man at her hearth she saw another young man at the same hearth long before, shining and stammering. But she quailed as she thought of what might become of Gwyn if he was caught up with the fairy folk.

'I won't be put off,' said Gwyn.

'Leave her alone, Gwyn. Take a girl from the valley.'

'I won't be put off,' her son repeated.

'You won't catch her,' said Megan, 'not unless you listen to me. "Your bread's baked and hard." Isn't that what she said?'

Gwyn nodded.

'Well, then. Take up some toes. Take up some toes.'

'Toes?' said Gwyn.

'Pieces of dough. Unbaked and just as they are.'

Gwyn followed his mother's advice. As night began to lose its thickness, he filled one pocket with dough, and quietly let himself out of the farmhouse. He sniffed the cool air and began to climb the dun and misty mountain.

She was not there. Shape-changing mist that plays tricks with the eyes dipped and rose and dipped over the dark water until the sun came down from the peaks and burned it away. Birds arrived in boating parties, little fish made circles, and she was not there.

Not long before dusk, two of Gwyn's cow lumbered straight towards the top of the dangerous escarpment on the far side of the lake. Gwyn stood up at once and began to run round the lake after them.

'Stupids!' he bawled. 'You'll lose your footing.'

Then she was there. She was there, sitting on the shimmer of the water.

Gwyn stopped. He reached out his arms and the

beautiful young woman rose and glided towards him.

The blue-black sheen of her hair; her long fingers; the green watersilk of her dress; her little ankles and sandals tied with thongs!

Then Gwyn dug into his pockets and offered her the unbaked dough, and not only that but his hand too, and his heart for ever.

'Your bread is unbaked,' said the young woman. 'I will not have you.'

Then she raised her arms and sank under the surface of the water.

Gwyn cried out, and the rockface heard and answered him, all hollow and disembodied. He looked at the lake and listened to the sounds, each as mournful as the other. 'I'll catch you,' he said.

'You caught the cows,' said Megan later that evening. 'That's what matters. You're not going up there again, are you?'

'You know I am,' said Gwyn.

'In that case,' said his mother, 'listen to me. Take some partly baked bread with you.'

Gwyn reached Llyn y Fan Fach again as day dawned. He felt strong and he felt weak.

This time it was the sheep and goats that strayed towards the rockface and scree at the far end of the lake. But Gwyn knew how nimble-footed they were. Even when one dislodged a rock that bumped and bundled down the escarpment and splashed into the lake, it was in no danger.

All morning, wayward April shook sheets of sunlight and rain over the lake and then, in the afternoon, the clouds piling in from the west closed over the mountain. Gwyn crouched on the smooth rock; the long waiting dulled him.

In the early evening, the mood of the weather changed again. First Gwyn could see blue sky behind the gauze of cloud, and then the clouds left the mountain altogether. The lake and the ashen scree were soothed by yellow sunlight.

This was the hour when Gwyn saw three cows walking on the water. They were out in the middle of Llyn y Fan Fach and ambling towards him.

Gwyn stood up. He swung off the rock platform and down to the lakeside.

And as he did so, the young woman appeared for the third time, as beautiful as before, passing over the mirror of water just behind the three cows.

Gwyn stepped into the lake, up to his shins, his thighs, his hips. Still the young woman came on, and her smile lit up her violet eyes.

Gwyn reached out and offered her the partly baked bread.

'Come with me,' he said. 'To the farm . . . I'll show you. Come with me! Marry me!'

The young woman looked at Gwyn.

'I'll not let you go,' said Gwyn. He could hear his voice rising as if someone else were speaking. 'I've waited!' He tightened his grip on the girl's hand.

'Gwyn,' said the young woman. 'I will marry you, on one condition.'

'Anything!' said Gwyn. 'Anything you ask.'

'I will marry you and live with you. But if you strike me . . .'

'Strike you!' cried Gwyn.

'. . . strike me three blows without reason, I'll return to this lake and you'll never see me again.'

'Never!' swore Gwyn. 'Never!' He loosened his fierce grip and at once she slid away, raised her arms, and disappeared under the surface of the water.

'Come back!' shouted Gwyn. 'Come back!'

'Gon-ba!' the mountain echoed. 'Gon-ba!'

Gwyn stood up to his waist in the chill water. The huge, red sun bounced on the western horizon and began to slip out of sight.

But now two young women, each as lovely as the

71

other, rose out of the water, with a tall old white-headed man between them. At once they came walking towards Gwyn.

'Greetings, Gwyn!' called the old man. 'You mean to marry one of my daughters, you've asked her to marry you. I agree to this. You can marry her if you can tell me which one you mean to marry.'

Gwyn looked from one girl to the other: their clefs of black hair, their strange violet eyes, their long necks . . .

One of the girls tossed her charcoal hair; the other eased one foot forward, one inch, two inches, and into Gwyn's memory. The sandals . . . the thongs . . .'

Gwyn reached out at once across the water and took her cool hand. 'This is she,' he said.

'You have made your choice?' asked the old man.

'I have,' said Gwyn.

'You've chosen well,' the man said. 'And you can marry her. Be kind to her, and faithful.'

'I will,' said Gwyn.

'This is her dowry,' said the man. 'She can have as many sheep and cattle and goats and horses as she can count without drawing breath.'

No sooner had her father spoken than his daughter began to count for the sheep. She counted in fives. 'One, two, three, four, five – one, two, three, four, five' over and over again until she'd run out of breath.

'Thirty-two times,' said the man. 'One hundred and sixty sheep.' As soon as they had been named, the sheep appeared on the surface of the darkening water, and ran across it to the bare mountain.

'Now the cattle,' said the old man. Then his daughter began to count again, her voice soft and rippling. And so they went on until there were more than six hundred head of sheep and cattle and goats and horses milling around on the lakeside.

'Go now,' said the white-headed man. 'And remember, Gwyn, if you strike her three blows without reason, she'll return to me, and bring all her livestock back to this lake.'

It was almost dark. The old man and his other daughter went down into the lake. But Gwyn took his bride's hand and, followed by her livestock, led her down from the mountain.

❧

So Gwyn and the girl from Llan y Fan Fach were married. Gwyn left the house in which he had been born, and his mother in it, and went to a farm a few miles away, outside the village of Myddfai.

Gwyn and his wife were happy and, because of her father's generosity, they were rich. They had three sons, dark-haired, dark-eyed, lovely to look at.

Some years after Gwyn and his wife had moved to Myddfai, they were invited to a christening back in Llanddeusant. Gwyn was eager to go but, when the time came for them to set off, his wife was not.

'I don't know these people,' she said.

'It's Gareth,' said Gwyn. 'I've known him all my life. This is his first child.'

'It's too far to walk,' said his wife.

Gwyn and his wife walked out into the farmyard.

'Fetch a horse from the field, then,' said Gwyn. 'You can ride down.'

'Can you find my gloves while I get the horse?' Gwyn's wife asked him. 'I left them in the house.'

But when Gwyn came out of the farmhouse with the gloves, eager to be off, his wife had made no move towards the field and the horse.

'What's wrong?' cried Gwyn, and he slapped his wife's shoulder with one of her gloves.

Gwyn's wife turned to face him. Her eyes darkened. 'Gwyn!' she said.

'Gwyn! Remember the condition on which I married you.'

Gwyn nodded.

'Be careful! Be more careful from now on!'

Not long after this, Gwyn and his wife went to a fine wedding. The guests at the breakfast came not only from Llanddeusant and Myddfai but many of the surrounding farms and villages. The barn in which the reception was held was filled with the hum of contentment and the sweet sound of the triple harp.

But as soon as she had kissed the bride, Gwyn's wife began to weep and then to sob. The guests around her stopped talking. A few tried to comfort her but many backed away, superstitious of tears at a wedding.

Gwyn didn't know quite what to do. 'What's wrong?' he whispered. 'What's wrong?' But his wife sobbed as bitterly as a little child.

Gwyn smiled apologetically at the other guests and shook his head; then he pursed his lips and raised his right hand and dropped it on to his wife's arm. 'What's the matter?' he insisted. 'What's the matter?'

Gwyn's wife gazed at her husband, and her violet eyes were brimming. 'These two people,' she said, 'they're on the threshold of such trouble. I see it all. And Gwyn,' she said, 'I see your troubles are about to begin. You've struck me without reason for the second time.'

Gwyn's wife loved her husband no less then he loved her, and she often reminded him to be very careful not to strike her for a third time. 'Otherwise,' she said, 'I must return to Llyn y Fan Fach. I have no choice.'

But the years passed. The three boys became young men, all of them intelligent. And when he thought about it at all, Gwyn believed he had learned his lesson on the way to the christening and at the wedding. He believed that he and his water-wife would live together happily for as long as they lived.

One day, Gwyn and his wife went to a funeral. Everyone round about had come to pay their last respects to the dead woman: she was the priest's wife, generous with her time and money, and still in the prime of her life.

After the funeral, a good number of the priest's friends went back to his house to eat funeral cakes with him and keep him company, and Gwyn and his wife were among them.

No sooner had they stepped inside the priest's house than Gwyn's wife began to laugh. Amongst the mourners with their black suits and sober faces, she giggled as if she were tipsy with ale or romping with young children.

Gwyn was shocked. 'Shush!' he said. 'Think where you are! Stop this laughing! And he slapped down one restraining hand on his wife's forearm.

'I'm laughing,' said Gwyn's wife, 'because when a person dies, she passes out of this world of trouble. Ah! Gwyn!' she cried, 'you've struck me for the third time and the last time. Our marriage is at an end.'

Gwyn's wife left the funeral feast alone and went straight back to their fine farm outside Myddfai. There she began to call in all her livestock.

'Brindled cow, come! White speckled cow, spotted cow, bold freckled cow, come! Old white-faced cow, Grey Squinter, white bull from the court of the king, come and come home!'

Gwyn's wife knew each of her livestock by name. And she didn't forget the calf her husband had slaughtered only the previous week. 'Little black calf,' she cried,' come down from the hook! Come home!'

The black calf leaped into life; it danced around the courtyard.

Then Gwyn's wife saw four of her oxen ploughing a nearby field. 'Grey oxen!' she cried. 'Four oxen of the field, you too must come home!'

When they heard her, the oxen turned from their task and, for all the whistles of the ploughboy, dragged the plough right across the newly turned furrows.

Gwyn's wife looked about her. She paused. Then she turned her back on the farmhouse and the farm. Those who saw her never forgot that sight: one woman, sad and steadfast, walking up on to Myddfai mountain, and behind her, plodding and trudging and tripping and highstepping, a great concourse of creatures.

The woman crossed over on to Black Mountain just above the farm where Gwyn had been born and where old Megan still lived. Up she climbed, on and up to the dark eye.

The Lady of Llyn y Fan Fach glided over the surface of the water and disappeared into the water, and all her hundreds of animals followed her.

They left behind them sorrow, they left a wake of silence, and the deep furrow made by the oxen as they dragged their plough up over the shoulder of the mountain and into the lake.

# Sea Tongue

I AM THE BELL. I'M THE TONGUE OF THE BELL. I WAS CAST before your grandmother was a girl. Before your grandmother's grandmother was a girl. So long ago.

Listen now! I'm like to last. I'm gold and green, cast in bronze, I weigh two tons. Up here, in the belfry of this closed church, I'm surrounded by sounds. Mouthfuls of air. Words ring me.

High on this crumbling cliff, I can see the fields of spring and summer corn; they're green and gold, as I am. I can see the shining water, silver and black, and the far fisherman on it. And look! Here comes the bellringer – the old bellwoman.

❧

I am the bellwoman. For as long as I live I'll ring this old bell for those who will listen.

Not the church people; they have all gone. Not the

sea birds; not the lugworms; not the inside-out crabs nor the shining mackerel. Whenever storms shatter the glass or fogs take me by the throat, I ring for the sailor and the fisherman. I warn them off the quicksands and away from the crumbling cliff. I ring and save them from the sea-god.

❧

I am the sea-god. My body is dark; it's so bright you can scarcely look at me, so deep you cannot fathom me.

My clothing is salt-fret raised by the four winds, twisting shreds of mist, shining gloom. And fog, fog, proofed and damp and cold. I'll wrap them around the fisherman. I'll wreck his boat.

I remember the days when I ruled earth. I ruled her all – every grain and granule – and I'll rule her again. I'll gnaw at this crumbling cliff tonight. I'll undermine the church and its graveyard. I'll chew on the bones of the dead.

❧

We are the dead. We died in bed, we died on the sword, we fell out of the sky, we swallowed the ocean.

To come to this: this green graveyard with its rows of narrow beds. Each of us separate and all of us one.

We lived in time and we're still wrapped in sound and movement – gull-glide, gull-swoop. We live time out, long bundles of bone bedded in the cliff.

❧

I am the cliff. Keep away from me. I'm jumpy and shrinking, unsure of myself. I may let you down badly.

Layers and bands, boulders and gravel and grit and little shining stones: these are earth's bones. But the sea-god keeps laughing and crying and digging and tugging. I scarcely know where I am and I know time is ending. Fences. Red flags. Keep away from me. I'm not fit for the living.

❧

We are the living. One night half of a cottage – Peter's cottage – bucketed down into the boiling water and he was left standing on the cliff in his night-shirt.

After that, everyone wanted to move inland. We had no choice. You've only got to look at the cracks. To listen to the sea-god's hollow voice!

Every year he comes closer. Gordon's cottage went down. And Martha's. And Ellen's. The back of the village became the front. And now what's left? Only the bellwoman's cottage, and the empty shell of the church.

❧

I am the church. I remember the days when the bellows wheezed for the organ to play. I remember when people got down on their knees and prayed.

I've weathered such storms. Winds tearing at the walls, flint-and-brick, salt winds howling. And now, tonight, this storm. So fierce, old earth herself is shaking and shuddering. Ah! Here comes the old bellwoman.

❧

I am the bellwoman. There! Those lights, stuttering and bouncing. There's a boat out there, and maybe ten.

Up, up these saucer steps as fast as I can. Up!

Here in this mouldy room, I'll ring and ring and ring, and set heaven itself singing, until my palms are raw. I'll drown the sea-god.

❧

I am the sea-god. And I keep clapping my luminous hands.

Come this way, fishermen, over the seal's bath and here along the cockle-path. Here are the slick quicksands, and they will have you.

Fisherman, come this way over the gulls' road and the herring-haunt! Here, up against this crumbling cliff. Give me your boat.

I am the boat. To keep afloat; to go where my master tells me: I've always obeyed the two commandments.

Now my master says forward but the sea-god says back; my master says anchor but the night-storm says drag. My deck is a tangle of lines and nets and ropes; my old heart's heavy with sluicing dark water. I'm drowning; I'm torn apart.

Groan and creak: I quiver; I weep salt. Shouts of the fishermen. Laughter of the sea-god. Scream of the night-storm.

I am the night-storm. I AM THE STORM.

Down with the bell and down with the belfry.
Down on the white head of the bellwoman. Down
with the whole church and the tilting graveyard.
Down with the cliff itself, cracking and opening and
sliding and collapsing. Down with them all into the
foam-and-snarl of the sea.

I'm the night-storm and there will be no morning.

&

I am the morning. I am good morning.

My hands are white as white doves, and healing. Let
me lay them on this purple fever. Let them settle on
the boat.

Nothing lasts for ever. Let me give you back your
eyes, fisherman.

I am the fisherman. I heard the bell last night. Joe and
Grimus and Pug, yes we all did! I heard the bell and
dropped anchor. But there is no bell. There's no
church, there's no belfry along this coast. Where am I?
Am I dreaming?

Well! God blessed this old boat and our haul of shiners. He saw fit to spare us sinners. We'll take our bearings, now, and head for home.

But I heard the bell. And now! I can hear it! Down, down under the boat's keel. I can hear the bell.
I am the bell. I am the tongue of the bell, gold and green, far under the swinging water.

I ring and ring, in fog and storm, to save boats from the quicksands and the rocky shore. I'm like to last; I'm cast in bronze, I weigh two tons.

Listen now! Can you hear me? Can you hear the changes of the sea?

# Notes and Sources

# Sea-Woman

SOME PEOPLE SAY CHILDREN WITH WEBBED FINGERS OR webbed toes are descended from seals. Seals have liquid dark eyes; they can weep, and their wail is like that of distressed small children. No wonder that the way in which so many of them are bludgeoned to death is so deeply repugnant.

In writing that for as long as seals live, 'their sea-longing shall be land-longing and their land-longing shall be sea-longing', David Thomson in *The People of the Sea* somehow comes close to the heart of my book. The earliest version I know of this story is 'The Mermaid Wife' in *The Fairy Mythology* by Thomas Keightley (1828), and it comes from Unst in the Shetland Isles. I've retold it as a tale-within-a-tale in which what the shell says really amounts to what the girl remembers, and I've drawn on my own firsthand experience of an afternoon spent in the company of a seal in Orkney.

# The Green Children

I THINK THIS IS MY FAVOURITE BRITISH FOLK-TALE. SO FULL of longings and questions, it tells us lasting truths about who we are, and how we long to belong; about intolerance and acceptance. It was twice written down in the 13th century – by Ralph of Coggeshall, the Abbot of a Cistercian monastery, and by William, a canon at Newburgh Priory in Yorkshire. They both say that during the reign of King Stephen (1135-54), villagers at Woolpit in Suffolk, near Bury St. Edmunds, found a girl and a boy 'green in the whole body' near the 'wolf-pits' from which the village takes its name. The composer Nicola LeFanu and I made a children's opera of this story, while here the green girl tells her own tale.

# The Wildman

SOME FISHERMEN FROM ORFORD IN SUFFOLK CAUGHT A wildman in their nets. He was completely naked, and covered in hair. This poor creature was imprisoned in Orford Castle and tortured but that did not enable him to speak or to recognise the Cross. But the strange, affecting thing is that when the wildman was finally released, he chose to come straight back in captivity, as if giving his human captors one last chance, before disappearing once and for all. Like 'The Green Children', this event was recorded by Ralph of Coggeshall in his lively *Chronicon Anglicanum* in about 1210 AD.

## Fine Field of Flax

WHAT IS A GLOUP? IT'S A CHASM AND THE ONE TO which the girl in this story walks is the Gloup of Root on the island of South Ronaldsay in Orkney. To my mind, what makes this tear-bright tale so memorable is the contrast between the clean, poor lives of the girl and her mother and the arrogant, dirty hypocrisy of the Church and feudal community who suit themselves first by throwing them out and then by welcoming them back. And the mother: is her daughter telling us that she was a virgin? There is a version of this story in Ernest W. Marwick's *The Folklore of Orkney and Shetland*

(1975) but, somewhere, there must be a much earlier one.

# Three Blows

I'VE CHOSEN TO END THIS STORY WITH THE LADY'S RETURN to the lake, but Mr Rees of Tonn, who first wrote it down in 1861, says that she had three sons, the eldest called Rhiwallon. They met their mother several times after she had gone back to the lake, and she taught them so much about the medicinal value of plants and herbs that they became famous as 'the physicians of Myddvai'. So, like the 'Sea-Woman', this lake-lady could not bear to desert her children.

There are many fine Welsh stories about lake-ladies (the Arthurian Lady of the Lake is one of them), and Mr Rees tells us that this one took place in the 12th century and that, until he wrote it down, it was told by one generation to the next:

> *The grey old man in the corner*
> *Of his father heard a story,*
> *Which from his father he had heard,*
> *And after them I have remembered.*

# Sea Tongue

IF YOU ARE ON A BEACH IN A STORM, IT'S NOT SO DIFFICULT TO believe that bells are pealing or tolling under the waves. There are stories about water-bells in Cardigan Bay and on the Lancashire coast, at Mundesley in Norfolk, and Dunwich in Suffolk where the sandstone cliffs have slowly crumbled and several clifftop medieval churches have fallen into the sea. Not at all long ago, my wife and I found a human thighbone, sticking out of the sandstone cliff. The source of this story is the Reverend John Tongue, who collected it from Norfolk fishermen in 1905 and 1928. I think of my 'fractured narrative' as a kind of sound-story for different voices, or for one voice taking different parts, and I wrote it for radio performance. Its form owes something to the idea that everything in our universe, each stick and stone, has its own voice.